LOVE AND LIES
CALL ME EVE

SANDI HOOVER
JIM TRITTEN

Red Penguin
BOOKS

Love and Lies: Call Me Eve

Copyright © 2022 by Sandi Hoover, LLC

All rights reserved

Published by Red Penguin Books

Bellerose Village, New York

ISBN

Print 978-1-63777-276-8

Digital 978-1-63777-277-5

Contents

Part One

Chapter One

She sat on the end stool closest to the lagoon, sipping a Fiji Moonrise, the house specialty at the Natewa Bay Resort's water's edge bar. The thatched roof overhead rustled in the breeze off the bay. She watched the darkening sky.

Well, that's swift. Sun crashes into the ocean without a breath.

Her shoulders slumped as her mood followed the sun, and she stirred her drink, staring at the line of white, lacy foam and listening to the soft murmur of waves. In the dark, they were the sole indicators of the expansive Pacific beyond the surf.

Coming here a mistake? Rest, and some recovery time sounded good. I'm not sure this is where I need or want to be. Hmmm. Cut my stay short? Go home early?

Her deepening gloom led her into the logistics involved in changing reservations. Her stomach churned, thinking about the difficulty and cost of changing flights to get home from Fiji's outer islands. She sighed, imagining complications, and weighing her options; she took another sip of the fizzy tropical fruit drink hiding a potent cocktail.

The bar with its open sides, Melanesian music, and flickering bamboo torches had, for the most part, emptied of vacationers and their animated chatter. Even the several couples who were drinking at secluded tables when she arrived had gone.

Perhaps to dinner, or off to their bungalows to enjoy one another. It's been so long.

She smiled briefly.

I do remember what the urge is like.

She grasped the tall frosty glass and took another swallow of Moonrise.

Bleah. I'm going back to my dry vodka martinis. This is like candy.

She returned to contemplating her lack of sex and a fulfilling relationship, inhaled a gasping breath, and suppressed gagging over the too sweet, tangerine-like aroma of frangipani somewhere in the darkness surrounding the bar.

Okay, enough of this pity party. Got a lovely bungalow. Pristine white beach. Clear turquoise water. What more do I need?

The answer to that sprang to mind, and she gasped again, shoulders hunched; as her eyes filled with tears, she fought to blink into submission.

Oh, Steven. If only I could turn back the clock.

She took a deep breath and straightened her spine as she exhaled.

It'll be okay. Somehow it will.

Composure regained, she swiveled on her stool and pretended to check the room, as if waiting for friends and expecting them soon. She hoped whatever emotion she might have shown hadn't attracted attention from anyone still there.

The tables near her were empty, so she continued her stool rotation. At the other end of the space, alone at a table on the ocean side, a nice-looking man was staring at her. He barely nodded as their eyes met. She glanced away and kept turning as if still hunting for missing companions, but she couldn't control her minimal, embarrassed smile at being caught.

Completing her surveillance, she ended up facing her empty Fiji Moonrise and the tropical hibiscus beyond the open shelving, holding rows of bottles. The soft sea breeze blew tendrils of bronze hair around her face, tickling her as she brushed at them.

"May I buy you a refill? The evening is far too pleasant to spend alone," an unfamiliar baritone asked.

She flinched at the masculine voice at her side. Turning her head, she saw it was the young man from the distant table. She hesitated, frowning, even as she noticed he was even better looking up close.

He said, "It's simply the offer of a drink. You don't have to leave your stool, but my table is also a possibility."

"Thanks, that's sweet of you. I was hesitating, wondering if I should have another one of these. But, yes, I would enjoy another drink, and someone to chat with." She stopped and smiled. "Sitting at your table would be more comfortable than these stools."

The bartender took their order, and soon they were seated at his table with a bowl of chips and peanuts to nibble, plus two fresh cocktails.

"My name is Mark Adams. I'm a lawyer, and that admission may stop this acquaintance right now if you agree with Shakespeare – 'first, let's kill all the lawyers' – but I hope you'll think that's a joke, and not real, as Shakespeare meant it."

"I got it. It's cannibalized from Henry the Sixth ... not quite right, but the point is made, and I'm okay with lawyers in general." She made a lengthier assessment while she sipped her drink.

Appealing and built like an athlete. Stylishly longer hair. Lets his curls take control. A bit of that stubble younger men favor.

Mark grinned. "Well met, but unless we want to talk in rhyme, we can dispense with Shakespeare. I'm on the way home to the states. A Japanese car maker insisted on a face-to-face meeting to finalize a deal. We're exploring the exchange of some innovative parts. Very dull, very boring, but crucial, according to the people I work for."

After a large swig of his *Yebisu* beer, he peered over the rim of his glass. "Now it's your turn."

She sipped her well-chilled, dry martini, taking extra time before answering.

What ... how much do I tell him? Just want a distraction. Something to fill an evening.

"Me? ... I'm returning from Australia – a medical conference on disease at the cellular level. You can call me ... Eve. My work is also pretty dull and boring to anyone outside of it." She studied her drink, stirring it with the olive pick.

This is awkward. Should I have told him my real name? Should I have told him what I do? Oh hell, tonight I don't want to be me. Tonight, I want simple.

"All right, enough silence. You're wearing a wedding band. Is your husband here too? I might as well find out now if this is just a one drink deal," Mark said with a smile and a twinkle in his eye.

She lingered on a swallow of martini before she spoke. "Oh no, he's not here, he's ... dead." She said, biting her lower lip as her eyes filled with tears. While she battled her visible emotion, she thought, *Where did that come from? But how true. Every day is a little death with Steven. Harder than one large one.*

"I'm so sorry, and I apologize. I didn't intend to pry. I'll listen if you want to talk about it," Mark said.

"You had no way of knowing. The wedding band still means a lot. I'm finding it hard being here – surrounded by so many couples. I think it was a mistake to come here for a little respite. The last time I was in these islands, I was one of those couples."

Eve swept a hand across her cheek to brush her hair back. She couldn't help noticing his broad shoulders and toned muscles through the lightweight tropical shirt, and his tanned legs stuck out the side of the table. "I thought some time walking on the beach, and maybe snorkeling, would be therapeutic."

"I'm sure it will be. There's no reason not to stay and relax. Solitude can be healing. If at some time you want company, you can feel free to ask me. I've made the same error of being a single here in a couple's world." Mark smiled as he lifted his glass in a mock toast.

Smiling at his offer of friendship, Eve raised her glass as well. "Divorced?"

"No, I guess I haven't taken the time to settle in. I worked hard in law school. Got picked up as an associate by a first-rate firm. Then had to meet deadlines and make my billable hours for years to make partner. Next on to the corporate world, but after the recent hyper-serious meeting in Japan, I decided to come here to reward myself and figure out how to reclaim my life."

"It is a beautiful place to contemplate life." She sipped her drink once more.

Well … interesting. Older than I thought.

Their conversation turned to the resort where they were staying, relaxation and sports activity opportunities, and Fijian culture. Discussing snorkeling and other things they enjoyed revealed similarities in their interests. Their talk lasted past the sweat drying on the sides of their empty glasses until they both realized they were famished.

They were late for dinner, so the dining *palapa* was nearly unoccupied when they arrived. Eve chose a seat where the breeze through the open building blew her hair away from her face. She had them move from the edge where she thought the wind in the thatched roof was too loud for easy conversation.

"Are you sure this is our final seat?" Mark asked with a smile. "We could try that table if you want," he said, pointing to another empty one nearby.

She laughed. "I know, I'm being picky, but this feels better. Okay, I'm settled here. Let's order before I change my mind."

They relished ceviche, with its mixture of sour lime, sensuous octopus, firm white fish, and chopped peppers. Eve choked and grabbed her water glass after a spoonful. Her glass was empty; Mark proffered his instead. Their eyes met over the rim of the glass, Eve's still gleaming from pepper-induced tears, and Mark's, under a furrowed brow, looking concerned.

"You all right?"

"Yeah, I can usually handle something spicy, but I was careless."

Thoughtful. This is an unexpected treat. Stop now? Well ... after dinner.

They talked all through an exotic meal of fragrant jasmine rice with mango, shaved coconut, and other fruits that enhanced the crab with fish sauce, all mounded on scallop shells. Their looks at one another as they sipped wine became more personal as the meal went on. For dessert, they had a luxurious papaya pudding scented with cinnamon and vanilla, whose combination melted on their tongues as they tried not to stare at one another.

They were satisfied with the food, the conversation, and more than a bit tipsy when he signed the check so they could leave. Concerned about abandoning her after she said she felt unstable, Mark walked with her to her bungalow. His turned out to be adjacent to hers – both located at the farthest end of the line facing the bay. He took her arm to help her as they climbed the few stairs to her deck and front door. His touch was warm on the cool night, and she leaned into him, delighting in his sturdiness.

"I'd invite you in for an after-dinner drink, but I have nothing in the hut. Perhaps a cup of coffee in the morning instead?" Eve slurred a little as she unlocked the louvered door.

"Please wait a minute. I'm glad I decided to talk to you in the bar." Mark pulled the door closed again, and Eve leaned against it. "I'm not above a good night thank you kiss, for a beautiful woman who's offered me a cup of coffee." He bent down and kissed the tip of her nose, and when she lifted her face, he parted his lips and kissed her mouth, softly and very thoroughly.

She responded with lips that answered his touch.

Mmm ... pleasant. Just a minute. What did I say about stopping this? Coffee in the morning? What was I thinking?

Eve pulled down her arms from his shoulders and pushed him away. "You'll have to go now. I need to sober up, and so do you. It's been a lovely evening, but ... "She was trying to finish the sentence when Mark opened the door again, turned her toward her room, propelled her forward with one hand on her back, and, leaving her alone, closed the door behind her.

She smiled, remembering how she enjoyed his touch and wondered if he sensed that while standing behind her. She heard him say through the louvers, "I won't forget the offer of coffee."

Chapter Two

"Rise and shine, Eve! Is the coffee ready?" Mark tapped on her door.

Ooh, my head. How can he be so perky?

Eve threw a thin robe over her sleeping t-shirt and unfastened the door while trying to smooth down her shoulder-length bob. His hair glowed from being backlit, making her think of saints in old paintings.

No saint ever had a bod like this, and jeez, he's cheerful at …

"What time is it, anyway?" she grumbled. "What are you doing? It feels like it should be the middle of the night still."

"Breakfast time!" Mark pulled off his sunglasses and looked her straight in the eyes. "Come on, either get up, or …" He paused for dramatic effect. "Those are your choices." he wiggled his eyebrows like Groucho Marx and smiled as he grabbed her around her waist and swung into the room.

Her robe flew open, and she grabbed and closed it, in an effort to maintain a modicum of dignity. She was charmed by his happiness and energy. It felt good to have someone take charge for a change. "Ooh, you are certainly bossy and pushy! So, I'm up. Just give me a minute to get dressed. How about a little privacy? Go! You can wait on the deck."

Mark stepped away from her and bowed. "Your wish is my command, beautiful lady." He put on his sunglasses and backed out of her room.

Eve reappeared after the few minutes it took to throw on a halter top and boy shorts, run a brush through unkempt hair, and stuff a lipstick in her pocket.

Their morning and the early afternoon passed in a blur of a restorative meal, swimming, paddle boarding, and talking nonstop about everything from philosophy to art, and what life could be. They discovered and discarded a ten-year age difference; were enchanted with mutual likes in music and movies, and their dislike of traffic, which he faced in San Francisco and – she admitted when he kept asking – she dealt with in New York.

Sitting in the shade of a *palapa* on the beach after lunch, Mark asked again about her husband. "Do you mind telling me about him? Did you travel much together? You said you came to the South Pacific before."

"I ..." a lengthy pause and she continued ... "I don't mind. It's all still raw, even though he has been ... was essentially gone for years. Some diseases are challenging to have, or live with, and any neurological disease is awful. It has taken him ... it took him, by degrees, which makes the loss harder. Before ... yes, we traveled, we had active vacations, we participated in the world."

"That must have made it hard to cope with. You were losing your life as well as the person you loved. Mom faced that with my dad, who had Alzheimer's, so I can understand a little of what you had to have experienced." Mark said.

They drifted into silence, watching foam lacework form and dissolve on the beach in front of them, in that languid time of afternoon when an alcoholic drink with a late lunch eases the day toward evening.

As he escorted her to her tiny house on stilts, Eve said, "Mark, I hope you'll understand if I would like to be alone this evening."

"I'm not surprised, and I do understand. If you want company tomorrow, let me know after breakfast. I'll probably be where we were swimming this morning."

Chapter Three

At mid-morning, she spotted Mark, smiled, and waved. His smile, in return, showed his pleasure. As they met, he stood waiting, not quite sure what to say.

"It's okay, Mark; I decided last night to rejoin the land of the living," she said. "So, we won't revisit our topic of yesterday. Life is ... and we go on. It's nice to have someone to talk to and play with. If the offer of companionship is still open ...."

"Absolutely. Let's make the most of this tropical paradise while we have the chance. Do you want to hit the paddleboards again?" Mark asked.

"Lead on, that sounds wonderful," she answered.

One idyllic day melted into another. When they weren't snorkeling, they were on paddleboards or swimming in the shallows. They found a two-person kayak and spent hours navigating the bay, watching fish and birds.

Fatigued after an athletic morning of swimming and a lengthy lunch, they found a shady spot on her deck and lay on lounges, close together, listening to the gentle surf. Mark reached over and took Eve's hand.

"Eve, how about something more than just talking this afternoon? I get that you're not ready for something permanent yet, but that doesn't mean we can't enjoy the now. While I thought during our first evening that you were beautiful and interesting to be with, it's only taken these few days for me to realize I'm falling in love with you. I really want ..." Mark swung his legs from the chaise, leaned over, and punctuated his request with the beginning of a kiss.

Her response startled both of them. She rolled over to him, curling herself into his arms, and answered his kiss with a hunger that overwhelmed her.

When she could breathe again, Eve smiled up at him and stood. "I'd forgotten how exciting a kiss and hug can be. I haven't even let myself think about sex for a long time. I'm thinking now, and if you've planned well enough to have brought protection, we ought to adjourn to the bungalow's privacy, such as it is."

"Well, I wasn't ... oh hell. I was hopeful, so yes, I'm carrying."

She led him into her bungalow, where they had mutual discovery time, even though the swimsuits they wore hadn't left much hidden.

Their consummation was an explosion of yearning that locked them together. Sobbing, with tears running from closed eyes, Eve gasped, and gasped once more, trying to catch her breath. Mark's chest was heaving with his effort to stop panting.

Mark saw her tears and asked, "Are you all right? Did I hurt you?"

With a last sniffle, Eve smiled at him. "I'm totally fine, thanks."

He shifted his torso to the side a little and took his weight onto one hand and arm. He used his other hand to brush her hair from her face and kissed her forehead and eyes, tasting salt as he found tears.

"That was beyond words. Don't move; I'll be right back." Mark withdrew and disappeared into the bathroom. He reappeared with a warm washcloth and wiped the tears from her face.

"That's just to let you know how beautiful I think you are."

He lay down on his back next to her. Eve squirmed around and snuggled into his shoulder, draping one arm across his chest. She closed her eyes and dozed off, listening to his steady, strong heartbeat.

Time faded as they pleasured each other, trying positions, laughing, and exploring.

Eve kicked along the damp sand, scuffing her feet, and leaving a zigzag trail at the edge of the surf zone. Mark followed a step or two behind; she knew he enjoyed watching her rounded hips swaying. She added a slight extra motion to the flowing, semi-sheer wrap tied over her two-piece bathing suit.

"Eve, who picked up whom at the bar? I was wanting to say something when I thought you smiled at me, but I swear it is all a blur since."

She peeked over her shoulder and gave him her Mona Lisa smile. "Why I was just innocently sitting there, having finished my drink, when I was accosted by this handsome man who was obviously trying to get me drunk by offering me a refill!"

"Now that's not fair. You know I was ... not trying to get you drunk, but, meet you – sure."

Her grin larger, she turned to him and reached for his hands. "Mark, it was mutual. I didn't realize it at the time, but I think I wanted you to make a move; I guess I sent signals, and you responded. We reacted to a need in one another. I've been lonely, overwhelmed – involved with complex issues with serious consequences. I needed human touch, and you, too, looked like companionship – affection – was something you desperately needed. Loneliness recognizes loneliness. I thought it could just be platonic, but apparently not. We found one another, and it's magic. Let's not question it."

He smiled and pulled her to him, kissing her deeply and holding her tight. "It's not just the sex, which is great, but it's you, your attitude, sense of humor, and interest in things we've talked about for hours. I've let work dominate my life for many years now, and changing that is essential for me since I met you. Life can be so much more satisfying than I have let it be. I can hardly wait to build something when we get back to the states."

She wriggled loose from his hug and stepped back to look up at his face. "Mark, let's go on enjoying one another now. Don't think too far ahead yet. Your attention and lust – yes, it's wonderful as an older woman to be lusted after – has made me alive again."

"Eve, you can call me your boy toy if you want. I'm not all that young, and you and I both know – we're old enough to know what we want."

He held her chin, so she was watching his eyes. "I want you in my life. You haven't shared much about your life, but I sense you enjoy companionship. I want to be that man."

She watched him take a few breaths as he was clearly waiting for a reply.

After pausing to collect herself, she replied, "That's very sweet, and yet, I can't move my career, and neither can you. We've had glorious days. Rather than plan ahead, let's finish this week with more things that make us happy to have found one another."

He grinned at her suggestion and dragged her to the surf's edge, splashing in the inch-deep water as the wave receded. "As I started to say earlier and was interrupted, your wish is my command." He bowed at the waist and swept a hand as if he were a courtier. Holding her hand, he proposed a few last things to do, including more lovemaking, as they continued strolling down the soft white sand, windblown coco palms leading them on.

Chapter Four

Will he go bald? She spread her fingers and fluffed his soft curls, then grabbed and tugged them as she arched her back in pleasure. She opened her eyes and glanced over his head at the breakers caught between translucent curtains floating toward them with the breeze.

The distraction of the surf was only momentary.

"Hold still just a moment," she said. Eve held his face in her hands and gazed into his eyes, noticing again they were as turquoise as the sea behind him. As she spoke, she also tensed all her pelvic muscles and drew them up inside her.

"Your wish ..." He stopped talking as her contractions strengthened.

She laughed. "You're free to move again."

"Oh my God, what was ..." she shushed his comment with a finger to his lips and rotated her hips under him. Their rhythm increased in speed and ferocity.

He ran his tongue around her ear and whispered, "We're getting good at this," as she panted and murmured in obvious delight. In response, she wrapped her legs around him and raised her pelvis more. Their movement became a violent rocking echoing the ocean outside.

"Oh Mark, oh, ooh yes," as warmth and tingles of electricity overwhelmed her. The sighing of the surf framed his climax as he rested more of his weight on her.

His explosions triggered more waves of contractions and sensual release for her. She wrapped her arms around him, pulling him tightly to her as they shared the intensity of complete abandon. After trying to breathe for a moment with him resting on her, she braced her arms under him to take his weight.

As she pushed against him, Mark realized he'd pinned her. He bent his head, kissed her closed eyes, nose, and lips, eliciting a smile as he rolled off her and onto his side, still panting.

"Wow – what an inadequate statement," he said. "Eve, you wear that sweet name as a disguise. Your moves are anything but innocent. That was insane." Mark leaned forward and sniffed her neck, coated with a combination of sweat, salt from the last ocean dip, and the resort's sandalwood soap. "You even smell delicious."

"You're not so bad yourself," Eve answered as she rolled toward Mark and drew a fingertip from his shoulder to his hip. "Why don't we see if we can stay vertical for a while and continue our walk on the beach?"

"Do you believe in destiny?" He asked on their return as they approached the stilted buildings. "Was someone looking out for us, or do they stick all the single reservations at the far end?"

"I can believe in coincidence," Eve replied as they climbed the few stairs to the little shelter she had at the resort. "But I think we create our own destiny." She pushed open the slatted doors on the seaside of the room, letting in light, more breeze, and the view of the ocean. "I just can't get enough of this. The aromas, the colors, the peace of the sea running to completion on the sand. It all answers a basic need ... but, enough seriousness. Let's find dinner and a cocktail, as soon as you go shower and dress too," she said as she rifled through the bamboo and rattan dresser drawer for fresh clothes.

Chapter Five

Trade winds carried the sea's rhythm around them as they stood at the entrance to the restaurant. The *palapa's* simple thatched roof was supported by hand-carved posts surrounding the dining area. The middle space was a circular dance floor, surrounded by rings of shadowed tables. Following the waiter, Mark and Eve were seated at a small table on the outermost tier where the dim lighting made their space intimate, and the room all but disappeared.

"I can't believe we've exhausted our week. San Francisco will be extra gloomy compared to what we've had here. You've made me aware I had shut myself off from things and let work take over."

"Mark, this has been such a happy time for me. So different from what I expected that first evening. Thank you for the rescue; I wish it could last." After the stimulating but overwhelming dinner their first night together, they learned to eat and drink without overindulging in order to savor their nights of lovemaking. They nibbled grilled fish and guava as the frantic Fijian dancers filled the dance floor with motion and fire. Some of the dances were uninhibited sexual displays, and Eve rubbed a bare foot up Mark's leg to show him it was time to exit.

Chapter Six

Mark was still thinking about her as his plane from Hawaii landed in San Francisco. During those long hours on the flight, he re-lived their week, reviving feelings he had forgotten in the overwhelming demands of his work.

The shuttle took him to his Tesla X, a perk of working for the company. His drive home to the outskirts of Palo Alto was occupied with ideas for changing his life.

I'm a lawyer. I could get a job anywhere on the east coast. I'll surprise Eve with a call when she gets home.

His excitement washed away the jet lag, and he bounded into his house after parking the car in his garage.

"Hello, Mrs. Thomas, where are you?" He shouted as he slammed the door behind him.

"Yessir, Mr. Adams. I'm here – been working in the library. It's time to dust and vacuum all those shelves again, and the photos and certificates need polishing too. How was your trip?"

"It was better than I thought it could be. I'll tell you later. Right now, I want to make a phone call. The library is yours; I'll go to the kitchen."

His feet echoed down the hall. He stopped in the living room.

Have I never seen it before? How cold. It's a designer's showpiece, not somewhere a real person lives. I just occupy space here.

He stepped back and took a better look at his surroundings.

Maybe the next owner will have a big noisy family to fill it.

The adjacent dining room was also a decorator's perfection, not a personal item visible.

This is what happens when you concentrate on making a career? Making money? Not living? I want her in my life ... forever ....

"It's time to make that change," he said aloud as he entered the kitchen.

He took a glass and filled it with chilled water from the Sub-Zero refrigerator. Like all the rest of the kitchen, it gleamed with polished metal, another reflection of a decorator's current idea. Mark leaned on the counter while assessing his life over sips of water.

Chapter Seven

Eve's driver with Capable Car Company was waiting as she pulled her suitcase to the curb. "Good afternoon, Ernest. Thanks for your impeccable timing. I was worried since my phone died, and I couldn't call to confirm. I should have known you wouldn't forget me."

"Ma'am, you are welcome. I'm always glad to drive you there and back again, and here's your Café Macchiato for the ride home."

"Thank you, Ernest; you remember everything." With a tired smile, Eve settled back and fastened her seat belt.

Having nothing to do but ride, she watched colorful trees slide by and sipped her coffee, hoping to revive as she imagined her impending homecoming. It was a routine always the same, but not unloved even so. It was vivid even with her eyes closed.

I will haul my suitcase to the door, be greeted by Martha, head for Steve's room, and prepare to smile.

She shook her head, imagining that stress.

Steve will be propped in his wheelchair with all the accessories necessary for someone who can do nothing without assistance. He will be angled toward windows so he can see the blaze of fall colors. I will find the strength somewhere to resume my true name and relationship – his wife, Michelle. Eve will be gone forever.

The tires rumbled on the grating as they crossed over the Whitestone Bridge, breaking her train of thought. Her movie played again.

"Hello sweetheart, I'm home. It's good to be back. You feelin' all right?" I will rub his misshapen shoulders, take a towel, and wipe his chin. I will lean over his shoulder so I can see the computer braced in front of his withered body. Moving into his line of vision, I will still be saddened seeing the remnants of the handsome man he had been. Today the old Steven lingered only in his eyes, a startling turquoise blue, reminding her momentarily of a recent tryst.

Ernest merged onto I-95, and the car lurched, startling her, and interrupting again. She continued her mental movie.

"Michelle, dearest, how was the conference?" Laboriously, he will breathe into the mouthpiece on the computer suspended before him to create the words. I'll wait patiently for him to finish the expected question before answering. I will kiss his forehead, see my love reflected in his eyes.

"It was worthwhile. Many renowned researchers. I solidified my contacts. Our foundation is helping, and we exchanged a lot of details about where they are in battling this damnable disease. So meaningful to be face to face, rather than trying to communicate by email. There is quality work being done, and I have hope."

"Tired? Enjoy Fiji?" Steve will force himself to make the words.

She looked outside the cab and blotted tears, thinking of her lie to come, and was surprised to see the *Welcome to Connecticut* sign fly past. Michelle thought of the reassuring words she would find to satisfy his fatiguing brain.

"Well, yes, and yes. Even with the week's break on the island, the trip was too long. Those are long flights and tiring, plus the endless drive from New York. You rest, and I'll unpack. I'll be back soon, dear."

Michelle held the business card she had tucked unread into her wallet. *Mark Adams,* his scrawled home phone unintelligible, as was the personal email written below the company account printed on the card. She shook her head as she tore the card into bits. Tears rolled down her cheek as she looked at the pieces.

I could reconstruct the number with these, but could I reconstruct my life?

She rolled down the window, held her hand out into the chill, and let the tiny pieces whirl away like snowflakes.

Chapter Eight

She shivered and tried to pull her sweater closer as she dragged her suitcase toward the door, balancing her purse and laptop.

What a contrast ... Mark an erotic dream? What was that beer he liked?

Reaching the top step, she rang the bell and took a deep breath.

"Oh, Mrs. Williams, thank God you're home." The housekeeper burst into tears. "Let me help you."

Hurrying made them awkward, but they got into the house as Michelle said, "Oh no! Some crisis has happened with Steve, hasn't it, Martha? Is he here? At the hospital? Where is he? Damn, I should have been here! I'll get my car keys. I need to go." Michelle rattled without thinking while pulling her cardigan tighter and shook with nerves and fatigue. "No, I need my coat; it's like winter here."

"It's too late. Ooh, Mrs. Williams, you didn't get my message?" Martha's voice went up in a wail as she grabbed a tissue from her pocket and sniffled in it. Finally, Eve noticed her splotchy skin and how red her eyes were. "Mr. Steven's gone. I'm so sorry."

Shaking her head, Michelle collapsed in the nearest chair, "No, no! He was okay – stable – when I left." Her hand flew to her breast, and she hiccupped in pain as she gasped. "I needed to be here instead of ..." she winced as she finished the thought. Her voice broke and quivered, and tears overflowed. She cleared her throat and tried to gain control, "When did he ... where?" She lapsed into silence while she fumbled for a tissue in her purse.

Martha kept moving from foot to foot and wringing her hands; "I found him this morning," she said, sniffing and blowing her nose. "He was himself last night."

Michelle stood, and they hugged. When they finally pulled apart, Martha said, "He looked like he was just asleep. I followed your written procedure on the papers and called 911."

Burying her face in her hands, Michelle sobbed as Martha uttered through sobs of her own. "And I called your cell phone and left a message since you didn't answer."

Michelle's whole body shook with the ferocity of her anguish. "My phone died, and the charger was in my suitcase, out of reach ... I should have been here; I should have been here with Steve. Instead, I was ..." another sob interrupted her "... in paradise, away from taking care of him."

Chapter Nine

Putting down his glass, Mark glanced at the note he'd been carrying. *Eve Johnson, (917) 224- ....* That New York City prefix made him contemplate with excitement the changes he was ready to make in his life. This was the woman he wanted to spend the rest of his life with. He tapped the numbers into his phone and tapped his foot while it rang.

A mechanical voice interrupted the rings, "The number you have called has changed, or is no longer in service. If you think you have received this message in error, please hang up and dial again."

Part Two

Chapter Ten

Mark put down his phone in surprise.

Must be a mistake.

He redialed; the unfeeling voice repeated the chilling statement. Staring in disbelief, he dropped into the nearest chair.

Must've misread her printing.

He looked at the Fiji Natewa Bay Resort's notepaper she'd used instead of a business card. Eve Johnson, (917) 524- .... He compared the number he dialed on his phone.

Mark rubbed his temples. He glowered at the phone and shouted. "We had a week of fun, fell in love, terrific sex, and now I got a wrong number? Are you kidding me?"

He sat in front of the uneaten breakfast, thinking as he held his coffee.

Doesn't make sense. Number not working.

You can find anyone online. He moved to the library and opened his laptop. He tapped out an email to Eve's address from the paper and pushed Send. A quiet ding on his computer, and the rapid reply to his communication: "Permanent Error. This is an automatically generated Delivery Status Notification. Delivery to the following recipients failed permanently."

Mark clenched his jaw. "Shit."

Okay, check Facebook. Everybody's on Facebook.

He typed every variation of Eve, then Johnson. Evie, Eva, Evita, Evelyn, Jonson, Johnston, Joinson. He found no one whose profile or photo came close.

LinkedIn. She's a professional; she'll be on there.

Mark hunted for Eve with the variations with no luck. He leaned back dumbfounded.

Twitter, Instagram, YouTube, Google+ gave similar results. His shoulders sagged. He picked up his cold coffee while he thought of why she would have given him bad contact information. Every reason made him shake his head. Why?

Mark pondered the question, rose from his chair to look through the receipts from his trip. There was the hotel bill. He reached for his phone and started an international call … +64-3-442 ….

"Natewa Bay Resort, how may I direct your call?"

"Reservations, please."

"I'm sorry, but reservations does not open until 8:00 am. How can I help you?"

"This is Mark Adams; I was there three days ago in Bungalow eight."

A moment of silence until the clerk replied. "Ah yes, Mr. Adams, I see your stay in the computer. Was there a problem?"

"Yes, by the way, I didn't get your name."

"My name is Shanelle; how may I help you?"

"Shanelle, I took some photographs of the lady who was staying in bungalow nine, and I've misplaced her contact information. Could you possibly give me her email or phone number?"

"I'm very sorry, Mr. Adams, but our resort has a strict privacy policy. We never reveal details about any of our guests."

"But she wanted a photo I took of her sailing to show her husband. She wants them to buy that kind of boat."

"Mr. Adams, I am afraid I am unable to provide you with any information."

"Can you at least confirm her name is Eve Johnson?"

There was another moment of silence. Shanelle whispered, "No, Mr. Adams, that's not her name. Now really, that's all I can tell you."

Mark gritted his teeth and hung up. He closed the laptop and collapsed in his chair. He slammed his palms on his desk. "Shit."

Chapter Eleven

S itting in the kitchen, Mark finished off a beer. He took a bite of his sandwich and held a third ice-cold can up to his forehead.

Why false information? Was she some sort of international thief?

Thinking over their conversation about her reason for being in Fiji, he remembered her comment about a medical conference. He considered scouring hospitals in New York City, but what would be the point? Her name wasn't Eve Johnson, and at this point, he didn't even know if she lived on the east coast, let alone New York.

She lied to me. Who the hell is she?

Foam flew when he slammed the can down.

* * *

Mark threw himself into work. His return to his office the next day helped his strategy of keeping busy to avoid thinking about Eve. But thoughts intruded at inopportune times.

Why can't I get her out of my mind? She made her feelings so clear. Why doesn't she want to hear from me? Abusive ex-husband? Still married? Fearful of my reaction?

A month later, Mark met his friend Nathan at Hawaii West, one of San Francisco's hangouts for singles.

"Hey Mark, you got plans for Thanksgiving?"

Mark winced. "No plans. Let me buy you a *Tecate,* and maybe after a few, we can talk about stuff."

"How's Tesla treating you? Still a new car every year?

"I've been thinking about chucking it and getting away from this craziness."

Nathan's eyebrows went up. Mark offered no further explanation, staring at his beer instead.

Over a second *Tecate,* Mark pondered his drink and took a deep breath. "What would you think, no, what would you do, if you met a woman, had a short but intense relationship, and then learned everything she said was a lie?"

Nathan stared at Mark, "Huh, like you've never done that? Is this a rhetorical question or something serious I should understand? Do I need to put on my attorney hat?"

"It's a stupid question. She's disappeared. Even if I blew off her lying, I can't find her."

"Okay, I need to hear about this," Nathan said.

"It's a long story; let's have two more."

Mark shared meeting Eve in Fiji and his surprise at the intensity of their relationship in such a short time.

Nathan looked at his friend, "Mark, it's time to find another. Why don't just you just move on."

"I know you're right, but I can't get her out of my head."

"Hey buddy, there's a million fish out there. Let's you and me go on the prowl. We never had any problem finding women and didn't care if they gave us their real name, did we?"

Mark shook his head.

Nathan asked, "Then, what do you want?"

"I wish I knew. It changes from day to day. When I remember how we felt when we were together, I want her, period. When I come to the end of our time and know it was a masquerade, I want answers to shut the book and walk away." Mark's pained expression said walking away would be hard.

"Okay, buddy, if she means so much to you, why don't you hire a professional investigator? A female who looks like Scarlett Johansson. So, if she doesn't find this mystery woman, you haven't wasted your money."

"Nathan, you're not taking this seriously."

"Lighten up!"

"No, really – what would be the point? Paying someone if Eve doesn't want to be found?"

"A PI could find information where you can't."

"Okay, say this investigator finds her. Then what?" Mark pondered. *Yeah, then what?*

Chapter Twelve

As the months went by, Mark's suffering showed. His fashionable stubble grew into an unkempt beard. Too long hair was beyond the norm. Lunches went from business-oriented to lone forays to Hawaii West in North Beach, where he watched Sonia pour shots and dance behind the bar. Even a good-looking blonde didn't take his mind off Eve or whatever her name was. His boss told him to take some time off and get his head screwed on straight. Mark asked himself the same question, again and again.

How could I have been so wrong?

Instead of easing, his pain grew. Nathan joined him from time to time, watching Mark sink lower and lower. One Friday at happy hour, Sonia spoke up to the two old friends. "I'm sick and tired of listening to you crying in your beer. You, with the fuzzy face, do you want this woman or not?

Stunned by this direct question, he looked at Sonia, and his jaw dropped. "I want her."

"Well then, why don't you do something to get her?"

Nathan added, "Yeah, buddy, I've said it too. Get off your dead ass and do something."

Chapter Thirteen

Michelle entered the living room, her footsteps resounding on the oak floor. Without furniture and numerous antique rugs muffling the clatter of shoes, the emptiness was startling.

"Steven, I ... I won't forget." Tears filled her eyes, blurring the fireplace and adjacent windows.

How many winters have we curled up here with a fire on chilly weekends? Reading together. Talking. Enjoying being close.

Sobbing, she grabbed a tissue.

Too many memories. Another couple can build love in this place.

She gazed unseeing through windows overlooking a large park. The noise of cabinet doors elsewhere in the house brought her back to the duty at hand. She opened the doors on a cabinet between the fireplace and the window wall. Kneeling, she saw something at the rear of the bottom shelf.

The old, crumpled paper didn't want to unfold at first, but she insisted and gasped as she read the title on the travel brochure she found. "Visit Fiji and Enjoy a South Seas Paradise."

Michelle's crying became a wail. Her sister, Kathleen, hurried around the corner and grabbed her. She clung to Kathleen while her shoulders shook with the effort of crying.

As Michelle's emotion diminished, her sister handed her a new tissue and turned her toward the patio doors. "Let's go sit for a minute, and you can tell me what brought this on."

The summer's warmth and the beauty of the setting helped. Perched on the patio wall, she handed the folder to Kathleen.

"This is the brochure Steve and I looked at when we decided Fiji was perfect for our anniversary trip ... before we knew about his illness. But that's not it. I haven't told anyone since I ... I've tried not to think about it, but I ... I can't leave the thought alone. This is killing me. I feel guilty when I think of it, and I can't stop thinking."

Michelle took a deep breath. "I met a man last year ... much more than an affair ... in Fiji." She leaned forward, hands between her knees, head bowed.

Kathleen said nothing but put her hand on her sister's back.

"I came home to find Steve had died. I've lived with this, and I can't stand it."

"Don't you think you've suffered long enough?"

"Ooh, I don't know," she stood and paced around the patio.

Kathleen stood in front of her sister with her arms out. Another hug opened the floodgate, and between tears, Michelle poured out the story of her week in Fiji and telling Mark her name was Eve Johnson with a made-up phone number and email.

Chapter Fourteen

In late August, Mark hired a private eye. Nancy, a solid, retired Marine Corps investigator, laid out a plan to find Eve. She contacted friends in the Embassy guards at the American Consulate in Sydney to find the medical conference Eve was supposed to have attended. They provided the name of the conference, the local organizing host, and its website.

Mark and Nancy searched through photos taken at the conference and posted them on the website.

"There she is!" Mark pointed out Eve to Nancy. It wasn't a great shot, and they couldn't read her nametag, but Mark took comfort in validating the existence of his mystery woman.

Nancy said, "I think the way to get this woman's name is to return to Fiji and do some snooping. A few greased palms here and there, and I can have her name, rank, and serial number."

Mark thought about it and asked, "If you lied to a guy, made it impossible to find you, and this guy contacts you anyway, what would your reaction be?"

"Depends. If I went to the trouble of erasing my trail, there had to be a damn good reason. She married?"

"Widowed."

"You sure the husband is dead?"

Mark took a sharp breath. "That was my guess; she's married and lied about her husband being dead."

"Wouldn't be the first time wifey got some on the side on a business trip."

Mark stifled his reaction to the former Marine's snarky comment. He forced himself to think about this possibility while he stared at the inert computer. "Even so, Nancy, if she isn't in a healthy marriage, why doesn't she just leave him? She said she loved me."

"Listen, the bottom line is she didn't want to be found. If someone came after me when I had made that as difficult as I could, well ...."

"Well, what?"

"Well, I'd either send him packing or start making plans to get rid of hubby."

Mark thought some before he admitted, "I can forgive anything if only I can see her once more."

"If you hope to get anywhere with this woman, you'd better clean up your act. A shower and change of clothes will be a good start." Nancy shook her head.

Chapter Fifteen

I n her apartment in Manhattan, Michelle paused over the computer keyboard.

Okay, make a decision. Contact Mark and admit what I did? My hesitation in writing telling me to let it go? That week was as wonderful as anything Steven and I had. It reminded me of the early times in our marriage. Discovering mutual interests. The excitement of compatibility. Awesome sex. I needed what we had and still love him for it.

The paper with Tesla's address was sitting on her desk, propped against a figurine of Buddha. Using Google to find Mark had been one of the first things she'd done after getting settled in the apartment. She glanced at the paper.

Well, Mark, do you want to hear from me? I've started this letter twice in the last month. And deleted everything. How do I begin? What can I say so you understand – before you throw it away.

She stood and paced down the hall and back, grabbed her purse, and left the apartment.

The elevator took her to the ground floor as she stabbed at her phone. "Kathleen, can you meet me at the park? At the carousel? Thanks, I'll see you there."

Thank God for my sister.

A beautiful late summer Saturday, but Michelle wasn't noticing. Kathleen bounded to her feet from a bench near the carousel and waved. After an intense hug, she said, "Okay, what's going on? You sound stressed and look like you haven't slept for days."

"Make that almost a year of poor sleeping." Michelle sat.

"Darling, you're looking anorexic."

"Oh Kathy, I still don't know what to do. The combo of guilt over Steven's death and guilt over lying to Mark is weighing on me.

"Tell me while we walk."

"Did Mark also think we had something special? If he was as much in love with me as he said before we left Fiji, he would've been hurt badly when he figured out I lied. I didn't think very far ahead during our week. I got caught up in the speed and intensity of our relationship, and couldn't, didn't want to back out. I didn't expect our connection and the happiness of living and loving again."

"Sis, you are a head case. First, you bury yourself in guilt because you cheated on Steve, who would have encouraged you had he known. Now you're wrapped in guilt over the guy you cheated with. Did you write to him?"

"No, I've started several letters and deleted all of them."

"Well, I can't write the words for you, but you need to get it off your chest before making yourself sicker. Come on, act on your feelings. I said that months ago. Go home and tell this guy how you feel, how you felt, and what the hell has been going on."

Back in her apartment, Michelle sat down, rubbed her right shoulder, cramping from tension, and started again to type.

This time, I'm mailing it.

Chapter Sixteen

In Palo Alto, Mark puzzled over the envelope's return address – Ms. Michelle Williams, a name he didn't recognize, and a downtown Manhattan street address with a postmark on September twentieth. Not the typical solicitation letter. He got donation requests, but handwritten was different. The writing appeared somewhat familiar as he looked at the weighty envelope sent to the Tesla Corporation address but marked for his attention.

Letters were unusual in his business life, so he was intrigued as he opened and read.

Dear Mark,

By now, you must know Eve lied to you, and there is no way I can tell you how sorry I am. In those first few minutes of meeting, I only thought to keep my real self, and that unknown woman you met, separate.

Shaking as he recognized he held the answer to questions he'd pondered for almost a year; Mark refolded the letter after reading those first sentences.

These open floor plans are good for working together but not for privacy. Waited this long for answers. What timing. Nancy is flying to Fiji tonight.

He took a cup of coffee and the letter with him to a nearby park.

Life was complicated with Steve, and I just wanted a simple evening to enjoy a lighthearted conversation. I knew he was dying but watching it happen by degrees was too painful. You kept me from thinking about it while we were together, but I knew it would only be for one week.

The letter went on, recounting her arrival in the States to find her husband had died during her flight home from Fiji – triggering unending guilt. She touched on her months filled with grieving and deciding to sell her house to escape painful memories. She regretted the time lost by not contacting him sooner to confess her deception so he wouldn't think it was somehow his fault. She apologized for any emotional distress she caused and would understand if she never heard from him.

I had to let you know there was nothing dishonest about the feelings and actions I expressed during our days and nights. The happiness and joy we shared were real, and I know beginning a relationship with a lie was wrong. I didn't expect to have more than an evening's drink and dinner. Please forgive me and believe I loved you in Fiji, and I am writing this because I still love you.

Michelle.

Her contact information was below her signature.

Mark sat bundled in his coat, the cold of the bench seeping into his seat and thighs. He needed the benediction of warmth. September in the Bay Area was never warm.

He reread the last lines of her letter, remembering conversations, savoring the laughter they shared over comedians they liked, finding interests in common, books they had read and enjoyed discussing. Mark stuffed the letter into the envelope as he weighed Michelle's explanation.

He called his secretary; said he was not feeling well and was going home. He shoved his hands in his pockets and started walking, a habit he had when wrestling a problem's details.

She's right; I don't want a relationship with someone who could live a lie. Michelle, not Eve. She should have trusted me and let me understand who she really was. Her past year must've been hell. It's been hell for me too. Gotta call Nancy.

Mark got her voice mail. "Nancy, cancel the trip to Fiji. Gimme a call me later and I'll explain it." He also sent her a brief text and email.

A second call was to his friend. "Hey, Nathan. You'll never guess who I just heard from. Let me buy you a drink and tell you about it."

* * *

After they ordered beers, Nathan said, "You got me here with a teaser about your female from Fiji reappearing after a year. What's happened?"

Mark started to give him a brief recap of Michelle's letter, but changed his mind.

"Here, read it for yourself."

Nathan kept a poker face through most of the letter but appeared pained as he neared the end. He finished and scrutinized Mark. "Well, what are you going to do?"

"I don't know. I'm not sure what I feel. First anger, now …."

"Do you want to see, uh, Michelle again?" Nathan asked.

"I don't know! If I don't care about her, why am I so unhappy about what she did? And why do I feel so damned defensive?"

Nathan said nothing, simply watched Mark.

"A piece of me is relieved to hear from her. And have her say she's sorry she hurt me. Damn, yes, I was hurt. I still am. It's some consolation she's hurting too, which sounds selfish and petty. But I'd comfort her if she were here. She had a rough time when she got home."

"Conflicted much?" Nathan interjected as Mark took a breath. "Try our old flip-a-coin trick. Heads you go see her; tails you tear up the letter. If you get tails and say, 'I'll try for two out of three,' you've made your decision."

Mark chuckled, remembering the times they'd used that in law school, and it always had landed them in trouble. "But seriously, I'm – not sure what's the best thing to do."

Nathan glared at Mark. "You're kidding, aren't you? It's written all over you and in everything you say. You've got to see what you two have left; if anything, you'll know what to do. Go see her."

Chapter Seventeen

Mark stood opposite Michelle's apartment building, debating what to do.

How will we begin again? Should I have called first? Does Michelle make love with as much abandon as Eve?

His head buzzed as he leaned on a tree trunk.

Standing here like a frightened schoolboy is ridiculous.

He walked down the block and around the corner. Finding his stride and his usual comfort in walking to solve a problem, he kept on another block, on around another corner, and more. He discovered a pocket park where reds and golds of oaks shimmered in the afternoon light. He removed his too-warm leather jacket – and felt his phone.

The way to find out if she's home is to call her. Then we can either meet somewhere, or I can go to her door.

He called the number in her letter and debated hanging up on the first ring when he wasn't sure what he'd say if she answered. At the fourth ring, he heard Michelle's recorded voice speak in a severe tone. "Hello, if you're a telemarketer, you can hang up. Otherwise, please leave your name, number, and a short message."

Mark said in a pleasant voice, "Hello, Michelle, if I may call you Michelle, not Eve. Shakespeare would tell you I'm worse than a telemarketer, but we decided once upon a time that lawyers weren't so bad." His hand holding the phone shook.

He heard a gasp of surprise on her end as she picked up the phone and silence for a moment before he heard sobs.

"Hey, that was supposed to be an ice breaker, not a heartbreaker."

In his ear, he heard a sob ending with a hiccup and a giggle.

"That's better, Eee ... uh ... Michelle, it's hard to get used to that name. I should've given you some warning, but I was afraid – don't ask me why."

"Oh, Mark." Michelle sniffled, "I hoped you would forgive my bungled start to our relationship. You were to be company for one evening. Just a drink, and maybe a meal. Really, I hadn't even thought that far ahead. You changed my world – brought joy and love back."

"I'll take that as a compliment."

"It's intended as honesty, not flattery," Michelle said. "The hell I've been through for months has taught that lesson well. Never anything less than the truth will do."

"Continuing in that vein, how do we take the next step in creating a relationship based on our real selves, assuming you wish to renew or begin something?" Mark's voice rose slightly, straining to sound comfortable with any answer.

Through another sniffle, Michelle managed a small laugh. "That makes me happier than I've been in a long time."

"God, it's wonderful to hear your voice again."

"Mark, we had something extraordinary, or I wouldn't have written my lengthy explanation."

"We did, or rather we do, don't we?" Mark waited as the silence seemed like it would never end.

"Yes. Yes." This time both of them were silent until Michelle added, "Just the prospect of building something with you means while we don't erase the past, we can set it aside."

Mark answered, "I'm not sure I want to set aside everything. I found someone to replace Eve." Mark heard the sudden intake of air being cut short. "I decided I had to meet Michelle."

Her ripple of happy laughter was one he recognized. "You're right; there are some things we remember vividly. Where should we meet? Halfway? Not Texas, perhaps Santa Fe?"

He leaped to his feet. "I'd like not to let months pass before we see if we still recognize one another. Can we meet sooner rather than later? I was wondering if you have a favorite restaurant near Soho where we could get a reservation this evening."

"What?" Michelle's voice was an octave higher than usual. "Are you in Manhattan?"

"Stranger things have happened in coincidences in location. Pick the time and place, and I'll be there. I hope you'll recognize me since I don't have a carnation for my lapel. Actually, I don't have lapels. Just tell me where to show up." Mark said.

Laughing, Michelle said she would be at *Osteria Morini* in an hour.

"Really? You're going to make me wait that long?"

"Mark, I need a shower first."

"I understand; I was reminded about grooming recently."

After they hung up, Mark Googled the address for the Italian restaurant and the nearest florist. They were not too far. He walked, humming to himself, smiling all the way.

Chapter Eighteen

Michelle called Kathleen and though she got her voice mail, shared her feelings. "Mark's in town, and we're getting together for dinner." She stopped talking to laugh aloud. "I'm acting like a schoolgirl. I'm so excited! I think we have a chance. Thank you for your insistence; I let him know the whole story."

She sat on her bed and remembered walking on Fiji's beach and daydreamed about a trip with Mark to a new place to create memories together.

Am I trying too hard? Oh shit, what to wear? The Osteria is sorta casual. Not this, or this. Just the New York black uniform? Not that. I don't want to look like I'm in mourning.

Michelle leafed through clothes in a frenzy, trying to make a decision.

After inspecting her options, she chose a favorite pair of gray leggings, with black, calf-high boots, and a classic sweater in rust to highlight her hair, shaped enough to show off her figure. Michelle spent a few minutes adding some eyeshadow.

Enough is enough. No more about how I look. How does he look? Have I exaggerated his incredible looks? Will we still be attracted to one another? Was it simply Fiji or something more? Time to find out.

She threw a stole in grays, rusts, and blues over her shoulders, grabbed her purse, locked the door.

* * *

She strode toward the restaurant and got to the *Osteria Morini* sooner than anticipated, before the hour passed. She was greeted as a favorite customer.

"Ah, good evening Ms. Michelle, are you expecting your sister tonight?" The young man inquired as she entered.

"No, Tony, I have a date coming. May I have a quiet table toward the back?"

"But of course. Let me seat you. What is the name I should expect?"

"Mark Adams." She smiled and added, "He's tall ... incredibly handsome ... and you keep your hands off him."

Tony put a finger to his lips. "Ahh, of course. I am pleased for you, Ms. Michelle. Would you like a martini while you wait?" Michelle nodded as Tony pushed in her chair.

Did I imagine Tony radiating good vibes as he went to the bar?

She texted her sister she was waiting and felt her cheeks warm. Not waiting for Kathleen's response, Michelle turned off her phone.

Her well-chilled martini arrived in short order. She glanced at her watch. If he was going to stand her up, she didn't want to know yet. Still a few minutes before he was late. Another sip of martini to give her hands something to do.

Why am I so nervous? I've known this man – intimately, in fact. That's not true. We were intimate, but we didn't have time to get to know one another intimately. I want to know the details. Is he punctual? I don't know. Would he let me know if he were going to be late? My phone's off!

Michelle was looking down, fumbling in her purse for her phone, when she was startled by a voice that raised goosebumps.

"You are more beautiful than I remembered. The name Michelle fits you. Graceful and just a little exotic, like these." He laid a stem of white Phalaenopsis orchids on the table. "It's nice to meet you again for the first time, Ms. Williams."

Acknowledgments

The authors are grateful to the members of the Corrales Writing Group whose helpful suggestions improved this story. Our thanks to the Military Writers Society of America (MWSA) who awarded *Love and Lies: Call Me Eve* the Gold Medal Contest in the category of Romance in their 2021 writing contest; and a similar thank you to the New Mexico Press Women who awarded it a 1st Place in their 2022 Communications Contest in the category of Novellas (40,000 words or fewer). Last but certainly not least, we are constantly indebted to our spouses Richard Hoover and Jasmine Tritten who encourage our writing compulsion.

About the Author

Sandi Hoover

Sandi spent her working career as executive director of the Houston Audubon Society and the Bayou Preservation Association, both active conservation non-profit organizations. A birder and naturalist, Sandi enjoys watching and analyzing the behavior of wildlife, trying to understand how they fulfill their lives. Her writings frequently reflect her interest in the natural world. Writing as an avocation has been filled with growth and discovery. She is grateful to the Corrales Writing Group for their thorough and thoughtful critiques which have helped her hone her abilities.

Jim Tritten

Jim retired after a forty-four-year career with the Department of Defense, including duty as a carrier-based naval aviator. He holds advanced degrees from the University of Southern California and formerly served as a faculty member and National Security Affairs department chair at the Naval Postgraduate School. Dr. Tritten's publications have won him fifty-three writing awards, including the Alfred Thayer Mahan Award from the Navy League of the U.S. He has published eleven books and over four hundred chapters, short stories, essays, articles, and government technical reports. Jim was a frequent speaker at many military, arms control, and international conferences and has seen his work translated into Russian, French, Spanish, and Portuguese.

Other Publications by the writing team of Sandi Hoover and Jim Tritten

Mirth and Musings, Red Penguin Books (August 4th, 2021), 110 pages.

"Enough to Kill," *between the covers: An Adult Romance Anthology* (*The Red Penguin Collection*), JK Larkin, ed., Red Penguin Books (August 15th, 2021), pp. 67-76.

Panama's Gold, Red Penguin Books (August 29th, 2021), 112 p.

Awards for "Love and Lies"

Gold Medal from the Military Writers Society of America (MWSA) 2021 Writing Contest in the category of Romance

1st Place from the New Mexico Press Women 2022 Communications Contest in the category of Novellas (40,000 words or fewer)

www.ingramcontent.com/pod-product-compliance
Lightning Source LLC
Chambersburg PA
CBHW060600100726
47907CB00005B/1458